Dear Parents:

Congratulations! Your child is taki
the first steps on an exciting journ
The destination? Independent rea

STEP INTO READING® will help your child get there. The program offers five steps to reading success. Each step includes fun stories and colorful art or photographs. In addition to original fiction and books with favorite characters, there are Step into Reading Non-Fiction Readers, Phonics Readers and Boxed Sets, Sticker Readers, and Comic Readers—a complete literacy program with something to interest every child.

Learning to Read, Step by Step!

Ready to Read **Preschool–Kindergarten**
• big type and easy words • rhyme and rhythm • picture clues
For children who know the alphabet and are eager to begin reading.

Reading with Help **Preschool–Grade 1**
• basic vocabulary • short sentences • simple stories
For children who recognize familiar words and sound out new words with help.

Reading on Your Own **Grades 1–3**
• engaging characters • easy-to-follow plots • popular topics
For children who are ready to read on their own.

Reading Paragraphs **Grades 2–3**
• challenging vocabulary • short paragraphs • exciting stories
For newly independent readers who read simple sentences with confidence.

Ready for Chapters **Grades 2–4**
• chapters • longer paragraphs • full-color art
For children who want to take the plunge into chapter books but still like colorful pictures.

STEP INTO READING® is designed to give every child a successful reading experience. The grade levels are only guides; children will progress through the steps at their own speed, developing confidence in their reading.

Remember, a lifetime love of reading starts with a single step!

nickelodeon
Shimmer and Shine
Six Magical Tales!

 Published in the United States by Random House Children's Books, a division of Penguin Random House LLC, 1745 Broadway, New York, NY 10019, and in Canada by Penguin Random House Canada Limited, Toronto. Originally published separately in different form by Random House Books for Young Readers as *Meet Shimmer and Shine!* and *Movie Night Magic!* in 2016, *Magic Carpet Race!*, *Magical Mermaids!*, and *Winter Wishes!* in 2017, and *Happy Birthday to You!* in 2018.

Visit us on the Web!
StepIntoReading.com
rhcbooks.com

Educators and librarians, for a variety of teaching tools, visit us at RHTeachersLibrarians.com

ISBN 978-1-5247-7278-9

MANUFACTURED IN CHINA

10 9 8 7 6 5 4 3 2

6 Early Readers!

STEP INTO READING®

nickelodeon

Step 1 and 2 Books

A Collection of Six Early Readers

Random House New York

Contents

STEP 1
READY TO READ
STEP INTO READING®
Magical Mermaids!

Shimmer and Shine dress
Tala like a mermaid.

Leah has three wishes.

She wishes to see

a real mermaid.

First wish of the day!
Leah is on a boat
to Enchanted Falls.

Leah, Shimmer, and

Shine meet Nila.

She is a real mermaid!

Nila dives into the water.

Leah wishes she
could follow Nila.

Second wish of the day! Leah, Shimmer, and Shine are mermaids!

Nila juggles bubbles!

Third wish of the day!
Now Leah can
juggle bubbles, too.

Oh, no!

Leah is out of wishes.

How will they get home?

The Mermaid Gem
will help—
if they can get it.
It is protected
by a sea monster!

The sea monster
is asleep.

Oops!

Shine wakes

the sea monster!

The sea monster
will not share the Gem.

If the Gem is gone,
who will visit the
dark cave?

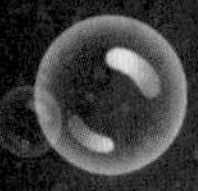

Leah, the genies, and Nila
promise to visit.

Shimmer makes
shiny stars
to light up the cave.

Now the cave is not dark!
The sea monster is happy.
She shares the Gem.

Poof!

The Mermaid Gem sends
the friends to their boat.
With the Gem,
they can visit anytime!

STEP 1

READY TO READ

Happy Birthday to You!

Shimmer and Shine
are throwing
a birthday party!
Who is it for?

Shimmer makes
a cake.
It is not her birthday.

Shine hangs
streamers.
It is not her birthday.

Tala puts on music.

Is it her birthday?

No.

Nahal blows up balloons.
It is not her birthday.

It is party time!
Leah comes
to the palace.

Is she

the birthday girl?

No.

Zac comes, too.

Is he

the birthday boy?

No.

Shimmer sets up
a birthday game.

Shine puts out

the birthday presents.

What a fun party!

But who is it for?

Surprise!

The party is for _you_!

Happy birthday to you!

STEP INTO READING®

Meet Shimmer and Shine!

Meet Shimmer.

Meet Shine.

They are twin genies!

Shimmer and Shine
live in a genie world.

Shimmer hugs
her pet monkey, Tala.

Shine gets a lick
from her tiger, Nahal.

Shimmer and Shine
love their pets!

Today Shimmer
and Shine get
to grant wishes!
First they must make
a genie bottle.

They mix
a ray of sunshine
with sand
from the beach.

Shimmer adds
a drop of water
and a cloud.

Shine tops
the bottle
with a star.

The genie bottle

is perfect!

The Magic Mirror
shows the genies
a girl named Leah.
Shimmer and Shine
will grant her wishes.

Leah and her friend Zac are at a carnival.

They see a game
they want to play.

Leah tosses a ring.

She wins a prize!

Leah picks
walkie-talkies
for Zac.
She is a good friend!

The man in the booth
lets Leah pick
a second prize.
Leah picks
a genie bottle necklace.

Inside a fun house,
Leah's necklace
begins to sparkle!

Shimmer and Shine
fly out of the bottle
with their pets!

The genies tell Leah they can grant her three wishes a day.

Leah wants
to tell Zac
about the genies.

Leah cannot tell anyone
about the genies.
If she does,
she will lose
them forever!

Leah promises
not to tell.
She cannot wait
to make wishes
with Shimmer and Shine!

STEP INTO READING®

Movie Night Magic!

It is movie night!
Leah and Zac
want to watch
The Dragon Princess.

Leah makes popcorn.

Zac blows up

their chairs.

The popcorn burns.
Zac's puppy, Rocket,
chews a hole in a chair.
The TV will not play!

Zac goes home
to fix the chair.
Leah calls for her genies,
Shimmer and Shine!

Shimmer and Shine
grant Leah
three wishes.
First, Leah wishes
for more popcorn.

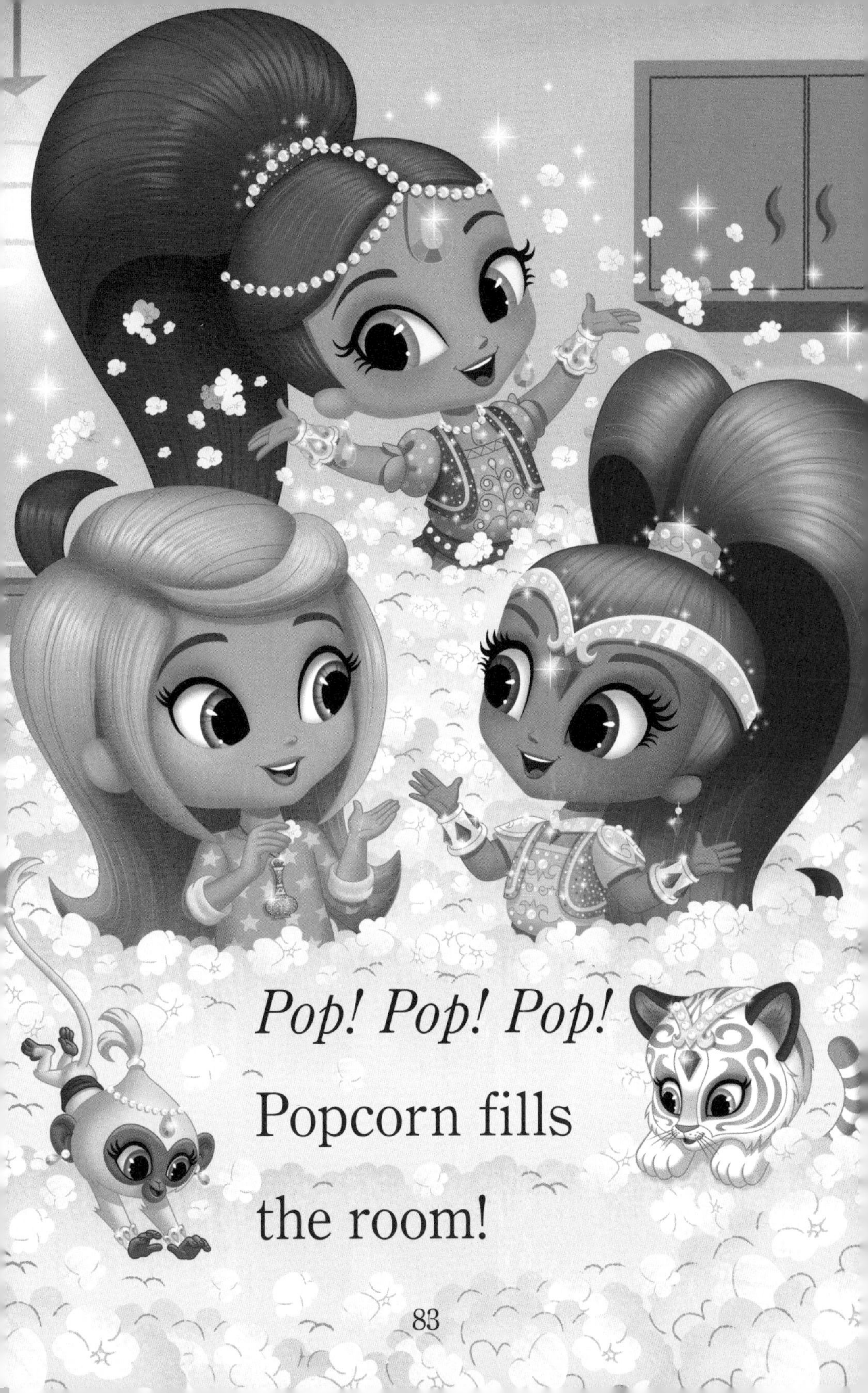

Pop! Pop! Pop!

Popcorn fills

the room!

Shimmer and Shine
made a mistake.
But it is okay.

For her second wish,
Leah wants to play
The Dragon Princess.

The genies think
Leah wants to *be*
a princess.

They change her house
into a castle.
Then they turn her
into a princess.

Oh, no! A dragon!
It breathes
green smoke.

Leah wishes for
the dragon to stop
breathing smoke.
That is her last wish!

Now the dragon hiccups green bubbles.

The dragon is hungry.

It wants to eat

Leah's house!

Leah tells the dragon

to eat popcorn!

The dragon eats
all the popcorn.
It flies away!

Zac comes back.
He fixes the chair
with popcorn!
He thinks the castle
is a great movie set.

Leah plays the princess.

Zac plays the knight.

Zac's puppy

plays the dragon.

It is the best
movie night ever!

Leah thanks
Shimmer and Shine
for another day when
mistakes came out great!

STEP
2
STEP INTO READING®
READING WITH HELP
Magic Carpet Race!

The magic carpet race is today!

Shimmer and Shine give
Leah her own carpet.
Now they can all race!

The genies and Leah ride to the starting line.

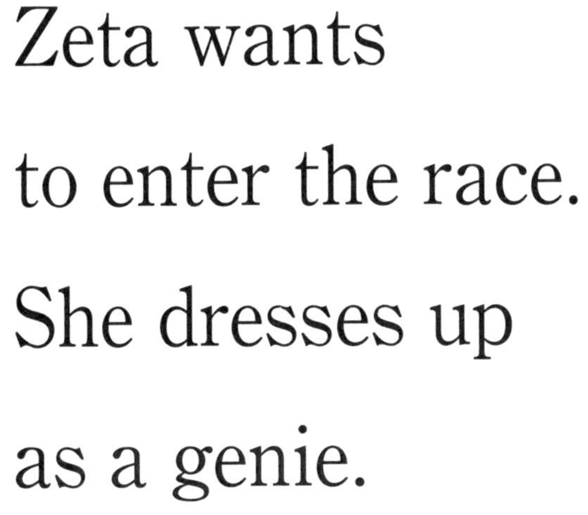

Zeta wants
to enter the race.
She dresses up
as a genie.

At the starting line,
Princess Samira
reviews the rules.

The genies must fly over the beach. Then they must swoosh through the market and zoom to the top of the island.

The first genie to cross the finish line will win the Racing Gem!

Shimmer, Shine, and Leah are ready.

Zeta is ready, too.

Princess Samira

waves the flag.

The race begins!

Oh, no!
Leah's carpet does
not fly very fast.

Shine grants Leah's first wish.

Now her carpet flies much faster!

Zeta leads the race.
She pours a magic
potion over the beach.

Twisty trees grow
and make a maze.
The girls are lost!

Shimmer grants
Leah's second
wish.

A sparkly path shows them the way out.

In the market, someone throws fruit at them!

It is Nazboo!
And there is Zeta!
Her genie disguise
does not fool them!

Leah makes her third wish.

Magic paddles appear

to whack away the fruit!

Zeta uses another potion.
The girls' carpets go wild!
Shimmer and Shine fall.
They land on Leah's carpet.

The friends need
to control the carpet.
First they swing
from a star.
Then they zoom to
the top of the island.

Next they bounce off a bottle.

Finally, they cross the finish line ahead of Zeta!

Leah, Shimmer, and Shine
win the Racing Gem!
It glitters and glows,
just like their friendship!

STEP INTO READING®

Winter Wishes!

One day,
Shimmer and Shine
build a giant snowman.

Their friends

Leah and Layla help.

Their pets help, too!

Zia and Neva

are ice sprites.

They want

to play their own

frosty games.

First, they race

on magic carpets.

Leah and the genies
ride above.
The ice sprites
ride below.

The sprites use magic.
They make
both carpets go faster!

Oh, no!

The pets fall off.

Leah uses a wish.

Everyone arrives safely

at the genies' palace.

Next, Zia and Neva
want to play
frosty hide-and-seek.
They fill the palace
with snow!

Oh, no!

Leah wishes

the snow away.

Then the sprites want to have a skating race. They cover the kitchen with ice.

Leah and the genies
chase Zia and Neva.
They slip on the ice!

Leah wishes

the ice away.

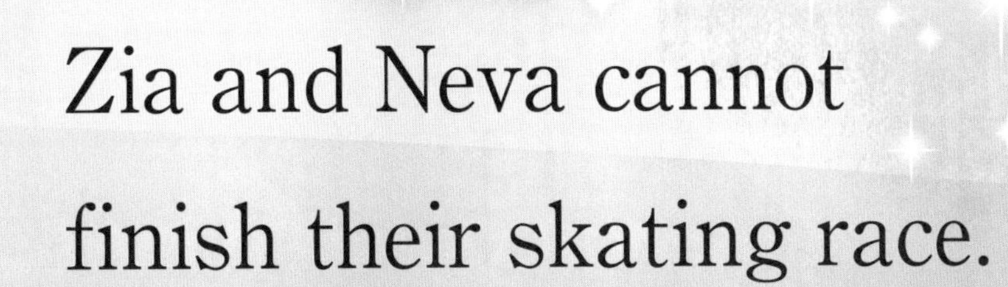

Zia and Neva cannot
finish their skating race.

The sprites
will bowl instead.
They make ice pins
and snowballs.

They roll the balls
and hit the pins.
Leah has no more
wishes to stop them!

The sprites make
a giant snowball.
They get stuck in it
and roll away!

The genies help.

They make an ice ramp.

The snowball rolls

up the ramp.

It flies through the air!

The genies make
a big pile of snow.
The snowball
lands in the snow pile.

The sprites are safe!

They thank the genies.

The new friends
team up and build
a new snowman!